Jimmy's Lost Bug

A retelling of
The Parable of the Lost Sheep

Written and Illustrated by
Simon Smith

Zonderkidz

Zonder**kidz**®

The children's group of Zondervan

www.zonderkidz.com

Jimmy's Lost Bug
Copyright © 2004 by Simon Smith
Illustrations copyright © 2004 by Simon Smith

First published in the United Kingdom in 2001 by HarperCollins*Publishers*
First published in the United States in 2004 by Zondervan

Requests for information should be addressed to:
Zonderkidz, Grand Rapids, Michigan 49530

Library of Congress Cataloging-in-Publication Data

Smith, Simon, 1966-
        Jimmy's lost bug : a retelling of the parable of the lost sheep / written and illustrated by
    Simon Smith.-- 1st.
            p. cm. -- (Clay pot parables)
        Summary: When Jimmy loses one of his pets, he keeps searching until he finds it.
            ISBN 0-310-70661-0 (Hardcover)
            1. Lost sheep (Parable)--Juvenile literature. [1. Lost sheep (Parable) 2. Parables.]
            I. Title. II. Series.
    BT378.L6S66 2004
    226.8'09505--dc22
                                                                                                    2003018667

Simon Smith asserts the moral right to be identified as the author and illustrator of this work

A catalogue record for this book is available from the British Library.

ISBN: 0-310-70661-0

Editor: Gwen Ellis
Design direction: Michelle Lenger

Printed in China
04 05 06 07/HK/4 3 2 1

For Shannon and Annalise

Down at the bottom of a long-forgotten garden, four mice were walking.

Jimmy was taking his
friends to look at his pets.
His pets lived under
the woodpile.

Jimmy had 43 pets.
Each one had a name.

There were . . .

Brian   Jack   Kate

Jess   Sophie   Caleb   Zoe

Peter   Luke   Graham   Hannah   Susan

Loren   Grace   Rebekah   Joshua

Sara   James   Jonathan   Max   Eloise

Barry   Harry   Caroline   Tom

Pamela   Mitch   Mark   Sandra   Megan

Gary   Penny   Rachel   Laura

Jacob   Joel   Tammy   Robbie   Daniel

George   Emma   Sam   and   Lester.

Jimmy took care
of his pets.

He gave them
clean water every day.

He fed them.

He cleaned them up
when they got dirty.

He gave them
lots of exercise.

"Here are my pets,"
said Jimmy.

"What are their names?"
said Big Al.

Jimmy told Big Al
the names of his pets.

There were . . .

Brian, Jack, Kate, Barry,
Harry, Caroline, Tom, Jess, Sophie, Caleb,
Zoe, Pamela, Mitch, Mark, Sandra, Megan, Peter,
Luke, Graham, Hannah, Susan, Gary, Penny, Rachel,
Laura, Loren, Grace, Rebekah, Joshua, Jacob, Joel,
Tammy, Robbie, Daniel, Sara, James, Jonathan,
Max, Eloise, George, Emma, Sam, and . . .

"Oh, no!" said Jimmy. "Lester is not here. He must be lost."

"Don't worry," said Stumpy.

"I'm sure you won't miss him much," said Big Al.

"You've still got lots of other pets left here to look after," said Bodge.

"I have to find Lester," said Jimmy.

"We'll help you," said Stumpy.

And the mice
set off to
look for Lester.

Stumpy looked
under the shed.

He looked behind
the water barrel.

He looked into all
of the clay pots.

He searched through
the weedy patch.

He looked around the compost heap. He didn't find Lester, but he did find a big shiny seed.

Big Al looked under the
scruffy hedge.

He looked behind the gate.

He looked into the pond.

He searched through
the long grass.

He looked around the brick pile.
He didn't find Lester, but he did
find an old metal spoon.

Bodge looked under
the rusty spade.

He looked behind the
wooden fence.

He looked into
the old bucket.

He searched through
the pile of leaves.

He looked all around the concrete gnome.
He didn't find Lester, but he did find
a long-lost toy soldier.

The mice were very tired.
They had been looking for Lester all afternoon.
Stumpy, Big Al, and Bodge went home to sleep.

But Jimmy went on
searching for Lester.

He looked all over the place.

It was getting dark.
But Jimmy kept
on looking.

He looked under the
roots of the old tree.

He looked behind
a rock pile.

He looked into
the broken pipe.

He searched through
the leafy bushes.

He looked around
the toadstools
and the anthills.

He even looked in the
muddy puddles.

Suddenly, Jimmy
heard a noise.

He lifted up an old
watering can and
there was . . .

. . . Lester!

Jimmy picked Lester up and rushed home with him.

Stumpy, Big Al, and Bodge were very excited to see them.

Jimmy's pets were excited, too.

"You are very special, Lester," said Jimmy, "because you were lost, but now I've found you. It's good to have you home again."

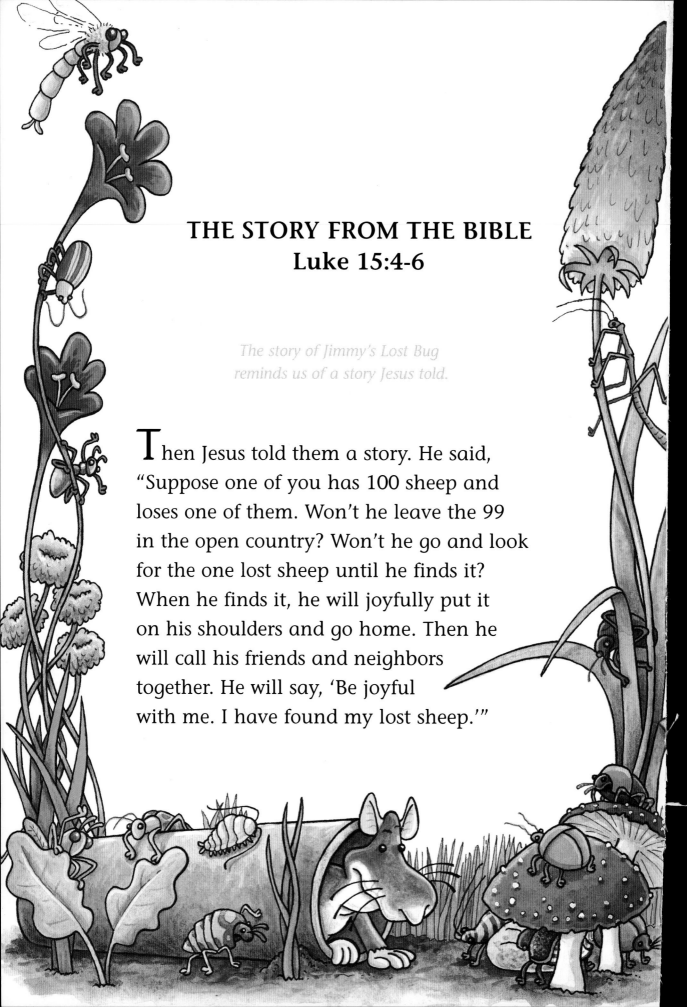

THE STORY FROM THE BIBLE
Luke 15:4-6

*The story of Jimmy's Lost Bug
reminds us of a story Jesus told.*

Then Jesus told them a story. He said, "Suppose one of you has 100 sheep and loses one of them. Won't he leave the 99 in the open country? Won't he go and look for the one lost sheep until he finds it? When he finds it, he will joyfully put it on his shoulders and go home. Then he will call his friends and neighbors together. He will say, 'Be joyful with me. I have found my lost sheep.'"